Santee Delta

Santee Delta

By Travis Teffner and DC Fidler

DCFidler Publishing
2018

Published by DCFidler Publishing
1117 University Avenue, #505
Morgantown, WV 26505
DCFidlerpublishing@gmail.com

Printed in the United States of America
by Lulu Press, Inc.

This play is entirely a work of fiction.
Any resemblance to actual persons, living or dead,
is entirely coincidental.

ISBN: 978-0-9989729-6-1
Library of Congress Control Number: 2018937594

Characters

- Colton Rivers – White male, mid 20s
- Jeremiah Lunsford "Luns" Planck – White male, mid 50s
- Angie – Woman bartender – White female, any age, preferably 40s or 50s
- Jennifer – light black female, late 20s, friend of Luns from NYC
- TJ (Tracy James) – White male, late 20s to early 50s – friend of Colton

Setting

- The Santee Delta Bar and Grill
- Luns' front porch and yard

Both settings are in fictional Port Indigo, a fishing village on the coast of South Carolina named for the wild indigo used for blue dyes that was grown for export during the 1700s. Fictional Point Indigo (Population 459) is north of Charleston, SC and south of Myrtle Beach, SC. The village is somewhat similar to McClellansville, South Carolina in appearance, but without wealthy tourists and wealthy second-home owners. Similar to McClellansville, there is swamp rather than beach between the village and the Atlantic Ocean. There is also a nearby fictional plantation, the Hamilton Plantation, a state park similar to the historical Hampton Plantation near McClellansville

Santee Delta premiered at M. T. Pockets Theatre, Morgantown, West Virginia on Thursday, August 21, 2014.

Cast

Colton Rivers: Travis Teffner
Jeremiah Lunsford "Luns" Planck: David Beach
Angie: Paige Muendel
Jennifer: Shannon Coombs
TJ (Tracy James): Sean Marko

Staff

Producers: DC Fidler, Toni Morris, and Vicki Trickett
Director: Sean Marko
Set Design and Construction: Andrew Amadei
Light and Sound Design: Mara Monaghan
Scenic Art: Sean Marko and Travis Teffner
Acting Coaches: Ashley Shade and DC Fidler

Note

In contrast to formal scripts for use in rehearsals, this is a book of the script, containing more stage directions to aid readers to envision what can be happening upon the stage. Most actors prefer few or no directions, allowing them to discover and create the lives of their characters.

ACT ONE

1. SANTEE DELTA BAR AND GRILL – NIGHT

ANGIE, behind bar, wipes counters, washes glasses, exits into kitchen.

COLTON: *(Offstage.)* Yer fuckin' dog! You jest let'im fuckin' run all over the fuckin' place!

TJ: *(Offstage.)* Shit, Colt.

(COLTON and TJ, carrying pool cues, enter through the pool hall door.)

COLTON: What I am sayin', askin' ya nicely, is to keep yer fuckin' dog away from my trailer.

TJ: Jug was tied up in the back'a my pickup.

(COLTON grabs TJ by collar, speaks in his face.)

COLTON: Not on my property. Not in my driveway.

TJ: He's a little pup, Colt.

COLTON: You want yer little pup to disappear into the delta?
(He lets go with force.)

TJ: Jesus, Colt.

COLTON: TJ! The Lord's name?

TJ: Got it ... What you got agin dogs? You's mean to all of'em.

COLTON: Angie!

1

ANGIE: *(Offstage.)* What?!

COLTON: Buds! So how many bags you sell Charles T?

TJ: Jesus, Colt.

(COLTON slaps TJ.)

TJ: ... Angie's listenin' in.

COLTON: She don't give a shit.

TJ: Two. Two bags.

COLTON: You told me he ordered a quarter pound now.

TJ: Charles T's short this week.

COLTON: Short?

TJ: *(Handing two bags of pot and money to COLTON.)* Wife and a new kid. I don't know. Truck payments. Short.

COLTON: *(Counts money.)* So now we sittin' on two extra bags.

TJ: I'll talk to him.

(COLTON shoots TJ a dirty look.)

TJ: I will.

COLTON: Angie?! You back there blowin' someone?!

(ANGIE enters from kitchen. She slams a case of beer on bar.)

ANGIE: Screw you, Colt. Cleanin' the mess that spilt outta the fridge cuz'a that idiot.

TJ: I defrosted it. Colt? Tell her.

ANGIE: And Santee swamp skeeters and moccasins bite only yer ugly ass.

(She serves beers to COLTON and TJ.)

ANGIE: Choke on'em.

COLTON: Hey whistle britches, we's Delta regs.

ANGIE: Ain't nothin' regular 'bout you, Colt. You is most "unnatural."

COLTON: And she wonders why we don't tip.

TJ: Ang is family's why.

ANGIE: Don't remind me, boys.

(LUNS walks up to window of bar and peeps in.)

TJ: Ya goin' to Flip's tonight?

COLTON: Flip's gotta ankle bracelet now. The Feds probably watch him from satellites or somethin'.

TJ: They can do that?

(LUNS enters, which rings a bell on top of the door. COLTON and TJ immediately place their hands on the knives on their belts.)

ANGIE: What can I do for you? Lost? Need directions, darlin'?

LUNS: Hi. Uh, no. Just want to grab a bite, that is, if you serve food.

ANGIE: We serve. To go, honey bunch?

LUNS: Okay if I sit at the bar?

ANGIE: Public stools. Fridge is broke so ain't got no salads. Got onions, hot dogs, burgers, catfish.

TJ: I caught'em.

ANGIE: Keep'em in the freezer long enough they don't spoil.

LUNS: Just a hot dog. Thanks.

ANGIE: No sauerkraut, no slaw. Chili?

LUNS: Uh ... plain.

(ANGIE snaps fingers at TJ and points at kitchen.)

TJ: I ain't on duty.

ANGIE: Five more minutes you is.

TJ: Then I quit.

ANGIE: And tomorrow you'll be down on them knees beggin' me to hire ya agin.

COLTON: That ain't all he gets down on them knees fer.

TJ: You ain't funny.

COLTON: Ah, make'em a weenie, Weenie.
(He play punches TJ's shoulder.)
I gotta go. See ya'll boys.
(He stares at LUNS.)
And girl. Have a good'un.
(He exits.)

(TJ begrudgingly exits into kitchen.)

ANGIE: Ya'll boys' manners suck! I swear!

(ANGIE leans on bar, calms, and smiles.)

ANGIE: I apologize.

LUNS: Accepted.

ANGIE: Drink?

LUNS: Water.

ANGIE: We got tap.

(ANGIE places glass of water on bar.)

ANGIE: Long ways off the interstate, ain't ya?

LUNS: I'm visiting a friend in Charleston.

ANGIE: Charleston? No one drivin' down the coast ain't never lands in the delta. Jest swampland here.

LUNS: I grew up in this swamp.

ANGIE: The Santee Delta? Now why don't I recognize you?

LUNS: My family died off long time back. What about your family?

ANGIE: My great-grandma's great grandma built the first shack in these here parts. Bare hands. Honey? We is this swamp.

(TJ brings out hot dog. Tosses it down, talking as exits.)

TJ: There.

ANGIE: From Port Indigo? Huh. Well welcome to the Santee Delta Bar and Grill. We just call it, "The Delta." Hot dog's on me, baby doll.

(She exits to kitchen as LUNS cleans hands with pocket-size hand sanitizer. He carries hotdog as he walks around grill, scanning room carefully.)

ANGIE: *(Enters.)* Somethin' special you lookin' fer?

LUNS: I'm a photographer. Way the sun hits old boards. Unusual color stains, paint.

ANGIE: Like a detective.

LUNS: Never thought of it that way.

ANGIE: That makes you the second one snoopin' 'round here this week.

LUNS: Did they find anything?

ANGIE: How would I know what she wuz lookin' fer?

LUNS: She?

ANGIE: Sometimes people look too close. The Delta ain't forgivin'.

(She exits.)

(Lights to black.)

2. LUNS' FRONT PORCH – NIGHT

LUNS, sitting in a porch chair, reads a magazine, cleans his hands with sanitizer, eats a few chips.

Sound of phone ringing.

LUNS: *(Answers mobile.)* Hello ... Jennifer ... I was in Charleston near the hospital, but I moved up the coast to my mom's old place. It's torn up from hurricanes, vandalism. Port Indigo, a fishing village in the Delta where they found Jay ... Still in a coma, intensive care. Sometimes I whisper to him, feel him squeeze my hand. I hired a detective but she hasn't found anything. The police found a few of his paintings ... A visit? Sure. I'd appreciate that. So would Jay. I'll take you to visit him. Gotta warn you, Charleston's no New York. But there is an art community. Good music, food, a few gays walking around holding hands. Black, white, Mexican. But up here in this shithole fishing village? One small bar, pool-hall kinda place. Last place Jay was seen before he was beaten. I rented a pickup so no one would see my car or New York plates ... I sound Southern? Shit. Hearing locals must'a hurled me back in time. This swamp's stirring up crazy nightmares ... Okay, text me with specifics. Don't want swamp monsters kidnapping you ... Seriously. We've got Spanish Moss draped in trees, alligators, white lightning, Ku Klux Klan ... I'm not making that up. Assholes beat Jay because he was black, dragged him behind a truck, left him in a ditch. Not one person lifted a finger. There were mean people in the Delta when I was growing up, there are mean people now.

(Lights to black.)

3. SANTEE DELTA BAR AND GRILL – TWO DAYS LATER – DAY

LUNS, sitting alone, drinks water, eats, reads photography magazine.

A toilet flushes and COLTON emerges, buckling his belt.

COLTON: Thought you wuz jest passin' through.

LUNS: Decided to stay a while.

COLTON: Why?

LUNS: I'm Luns. Pleasure to meet you.

(LUNS extends hand but COLTON does not shake.)

COLTON: Yeah. I seen you drivin' 'round in yer shiny new F-150.

LUNS: And I've seen you walking around.

COLTON: Yer always alone.

LUNS: I am.

COLTON: Fer what?

LUNS: Magazine photography.

COLTON: Which magazine?

LUNS: Have a seat.

(COLTON continues to stand.)

COLTON: Which magazine?

LUNS: Magazines you probably never heard of.

COLTON: What're you tryin' to say?

LUNS: Most people haven't heard of the magazines accepting my photos. Spain, Czech Republic, Thailand. Overseas. One photo in Newsweek. Long time ago. Join me.

COLTON: I'm waitin' fer my boys. Reckon I could down one cold one.

LUNS: Who are your boys?

COLTON: *(Overlapping LUNS.)* Angie!

ANGIE: *(Offstage.)* What?!

COLTON: Git yer ass in here and git me a Bud! Now!

ANGIE: Hold your horses!

COLTON: Women ... I'll git it myself.
(He reaches over the bar as ANGIE enters and slaps his hand.)

ANGIE: God almighty. You know that ain't allowed.

COLTON: One fer this fella too now.

(COLTON reaches over bar again, gets second beer, and quickly steps back to dodge ANGIE'S swing. He gives it to LUNS.)

LUNS: Uh ...

COLTON: It's okay. My treat ole fellow.

(ANGIE exits into kitchen.)

LUNS: I haven't had a beer in ... Thank you.

COLTON: Thanks Angie! ... No "Yer welcome, Colt." Rude bitch.

LUNS: You two seem to know one another well.

COLTON: Cousins ... Distant ... What'chu photograph?

LUNS: Mountain climbing, sailing, spelunking. That's caving.

COLTON: I know. You take me fer a fuckin' idiot.

LUNS: A lot of people don't know what spelunking is.

COLTON: Women?

LUNS: Men and women. What do you do?

COLTON: I don't work boats. I git seasick.

LUNS: That could be rough in a fishing village.

COLTON: Like livin' on a ranch somewheres and bein' allergic to cows.

LUNS: Or being an outdoor photographer and having asthma.
(He holds up an inhaler and takes a breath.)

COLTON: Shit.

LUNS: So you can't do boats. What can you do?

COLTON: Mow yards, clean gutters, paint.

LUNS: I'm fixing up an old house over on Hoory Alley.

COLTON: The old Planck place?

LUNS: Indeed.

COLTON: Fuck ton'a hurricane damage. I say tear it down and start from scratch. Hell-uv-a lot cheaper.

LUNS: I grew up there.

COLTON: No shit?

LUNS: True shit.

COLTON: You a Planck?

LUNS: Indeed. "Old lady Planck" was my mom.

COLTON: Ho-ly-fuck. Hey Angie! This fella's a Planck!

ANGIE: *(Offstage.)* I know that block head!

COLTON: Yer ... yer uh ... what's his face.

LUNS: Luns.

COLTON: Luns Planck?

LUNS: Jeremiah Lunsford Planck.

COLTON: Jeremiah Lunsford ... Jeremy, Jeremy ... Oh! Jeremy. Jeremy Planck. Angie! This is the asshole mom had a crush on in High School! Mom used to go on and on. Talk crazy shit 'bout you.

LUNS: Your mom?

COLTON: Rivers. Amelia Rivers?

LUNS: Amelia?

COLTON: Senior year. Had'er leg in a cast two months.

LUNS: Oh! Amy. Amy Rivers.

COLTON: Yep.

LUNS: Oh my gosh. A-My-Ri-Vers ... So you're Colt. Colton Rivers.

COLTON: Yep. You two dated.

LUNS: What?! Uh ... no, no.

COLTON: Said ya'll dated. Took'er dancin'.

LUNS: Dancing? ... Oh. Once. Sadie Hawkins' Day Dance. The girl asks the—

COLTON: Asks the boy. We had'em too. Two girls asked me. Two ugly girls. I weren't goin' with'em drunk or not. In fact I couldn't git that drunk. But you took my mom.

LUNS: I barely remember. She got me drunk.

COLTON: She sure as hell remembers it. Her dream moment in yer mama's car. Can't figure out why you never asked her back out.

LUNS: I left. Got accepted to a private school. My mother's car?

COLTON: Uh huh. She used to say you were her soulmate. Made sure her husband knew it.

LUNS: Husband? So your stepfather?

(COLTON shuts down.)

LUNS: Sorry. None of my business ... How is your mother?

COLTON: Same ole Rivers' woman.

LUNS: Not sure what that means.

COLTON: Jest got outta rehab. Agin.

LUNS: Oh ... Sad to hear that. That she was in rehab. Had to be in rehab.

COLTON: Yep.
(He chugs remainder of beer, burps.)
Where are those sons-a-bitches? Fishin'? Whatever. Well, I ain't waitin' all fuckin' day fer'em.
(He slams money on bar.)
Angie! Money's on the bar! The nickel's yers!
(He walks toward exit.)

LUNS: Nice to meet you, Colton.

COLTON: Hmm. You too, Jeremy.

LUNS: Luns.

COLTON: Right. Luns.
(He walks a few steps.)

LUNS: Colton? I could use your help with my house. I'd pay you of course.

COLTON: I'll think about it.
(He exits.)

(ANGIE enters.)

ANGIE: I got other kin hell-uv-a lot better than that one.

LUNS: Why? He's no good?

ANGIE: Colton there's 'bout as mean as they come.

LUNS: In what way?

ANGIE: You still playin' detective?

LUNS: I've been away from this place a long time. Not sure how to judge people down here.

ANGIE: A city slicker now, huh? What city?

LUNS: Now looks who's being the detective. Does Colton like to fight?

ANGIE: If I bragged 'bout my regulars, what kinda business woman would that make me? They're jest loud shit talkers. But don't cross'em.
(She exits to kitchen.)

(LUNS reaches over bar and pours his beer into the sink. He places two dollar bills on bar beneath the beer bottle and exits.)

(Lights to black)

4. SANTEE DELTA BAR AND GRILL – TWO DAYS LATER – NIGHT

ANGIE, standing behind bar, washes, dries, stacks glasses while COLTON and TJ play darts.

COLTON: You did not.

TJ: Did too.

COLTON: Hey Angie? You hear this shit TJ's talkin'?

TJ: Colt! Sssh!

COLTON: TJ claims yer sister gave him a BJ under the George Washington Oak. While a third grade class wuz climbin' up the plantation steps.

TJ: Sex Ed 101 live action!

ANGIE: Jest a BJ? Them third-graders could'a learnt ya where to stick it.

COLTON: Owww! You been burned, boy.

TJ: Hold on now. This wuz at my great, great, great granddaddy's plantation. I got aristocracy blood rights ya know.

COLTON: Bastard blood rights. I got Santee Injun blood rights. We wuz here first.

TJ: I forgit yer injun. Not American.

COLTON: Fuckin' retard.

TJ: What the fuck ever. Move outta my way.

(TJ throws dart and misses.)

COLTON: Damn, you can't hit that neither.

TJ: I know who I could hit.

(COLTON grabs TJ and holds a dart against his throat.)

COLTON: Who thin dick?

ANGIE: Colt? ... Colt?

COLTON: Thought so.

(Just as abruptly, COLTON retracts dart, pauses, breaks into laughter, talks in eerily calm, overly friendly manner.)

COLTON: Hey buddy. Still your turn now. You git three throws. Hey Angie? Wrestle up a couple more Buds for me and thin dick here now.

(TJ shakes head, resumes dart game, but is anxious and misses.)

COLTON: I'm feeling generous. Take that shot over.

(TJ retrieves dart. ANGIE brings beers to TJ and COLTON. LUNS stops outside window while he is texting. ANGIE sees LUNS outside.)

ANGIE: *(Whispers.)* Hey Colt. Yer new boyfriend's here.

TJ: That's the guy who come in fer the hot dog. Least yer boyfriend's white this time.

(COLTON knocks TJ's beer over with purpose.)

COLTON: Clean it up!

TJ: Fuck you, Colt.

(ANGIE tosses a rag to TJ.)

TJ: I swear.

(TJ gets down on his knees and wipes up spill. LUNS enters and goes to bar and reads magazine.)

ANGIE: Corona, honey? I know Bud's not yer style. Or would you prefer a Blue Moon? Got a few left.

LUNS: Blue Moon? No thanks. Corona.

ANGIE: I'll put a lime in it fer ya.

LUNS: Thank you.

COLTON: Mr. Planck? When is it I start that job now?

TJ: Job?

LUNS: What? ... Oh job. Yeah, uh ... what about when I get back from Charleston?

ANGIE: Why you goin' to Charleston?

LUNS: Photograph the Old Battery Area.

TJ: What kinda job?

COLTON: Thought we agreed I start Thursday.

LUNS: Thursday? ... Oh yeah. Thursday. Like we agreed. Uh huh.

COLTON: My boss man here does Spanish magazine photography.

ANGIE: Colton Rivers. You are so fulla shit.

COLTON: Better than what yer full of. Who yer full of.

(TJ carefully aims, throws dart and misses.)

TJ: Fuck.

COLTON: Don't choke thin—
(Coughs to disguise word, "dick.").
Remember this one's fer the whole day's tab.

(TJ throws dart and misses.)

COLTON: Shit TJ. You done bought me drinks all month, buddy. Sure do appreciate it now. Not enough to give you head under Washington's Oak. That's what cousins are fer.

(ANGIE shoots her middle finger at COLTON, who pretends to catch "it" and put "it" in his pocket.)

COLTON: Save that one fer later. See ya Thursday, Mr. Boss Man.

(COLTON exits. TJ reaches for wallet.)

TJ: Shit. Ain't got my wallet. Put it on my tab.

(TJ looks at LUNS' magazine cover as LUNS reads.)

TJ: Is that really Spanish photography?

(LUNS turns inside of magazine toward TJ.)

LUNS: Bobo.

TJ: Yeah. Nice.

(Lights to black.)

5. LUNS' FRONT PORCH – MORNING

On porch is a bunched up sheet of plastic, a roll of screen wire, and old jumper cables.

LUNS, sitting on porch, drinks coffee as reads paper, takes puff of inhaler, cleans hands with pocket sanitizer, breaks a bagel in half and takes a bite. COLTON enters from yard, wearing a tool belt and carrying a small cooler.

LUNS: Not only did you show up, you showed up on time.

COLTON: You take me fer an idiot and a bullshitter?

LUNS: Bullshitter? Indeed.

COLTON: Well I'm here.

LUNS: Coffee?

COLTON: Nah. Dip?
    (He holds out can of snuff.)

LUNS: A dip?!

COLTON: Oh that's right. You're an international photographer. Marlboro?

LUNS: I quit two decades ago. You dip and smoke?

COLTON: I started dippin' so I could quit smokin'.

LUNS: And now you do both?

COLTON: Is this why the fuck I'm here?

LUNS: Let's get to it. Hurricane did a lot of damage.

(COLTON spits a dip in yard.)

LUNS: Uh ... would you mind not spitting in my yard?

(COLTON gets Mt. Dew bottle out of cooler, empties remainder of drink into yard, spits into the bottle.)

COLTON: Let's start with this here porch.

LUNS: Right. Painting.

COLTON: Fix holes, sand, then paint.

LUNS: That's what I meant.

(COLTON measures porch floor boards with tape measure.)

COLTON: You got two by fours?

LUNS: Uh, not yet.

COLTON: Wy I ain't the one with no truck now.

LUNS: How many two by fours?

COLTON: Start with three dozen six-footers. You got a back porch?

LUNS: Same size as the front porch.

COLTON: Six dozen six-footers, sand paper, screws not nails.

LUNS: What do you take me for? An idiot?

COLTON: "Indeed."

(LUNS walks toward truck.)

COLTON: And paint. Four gallons to start.

LUNS: White for porch.

COLTON: And fer them shutters?

(COLTON scrapes a bit of old burgundy paint from the shutter onto the tip of his knife. He walks to LUNS with knife blade pointed toward LUNS. LUNS cautiously lifts paint chip from tip of knife and exits through yard.)

(COLTON pulls off shirt, throws sheet of plastic and jumper cables into yard, finds radio underneath. Turns radio on, tunes it to country station, sings along. Opens cooler, gets a Bud beer and drinks. He smells LUN'S coffee, grimaces, tosses coffee into yard.)

(JENNIFER enters the yard, wearing sunglasses, dressed in sophisticated New York City casual clothes, towing a suitcase. She pauses at edge of yard, looks at notecard. COLTON sees her and turns off radio.)

COLTON: Well now. Who might you be?

JENNIFER: This is 214 Horry Alley?

(COLTON brushes off hanging moss covering street number on porch post.)

COLTON: Yep.

JENNIFER: You know Lunsford Planck?

COLTON: Yep.

JENNIFER: Well, I'm visiting him.

COLTON: Well, I'm fixin' up his place.

JENNIFER: Is he inside?

COLTON: Nope.

JENNIFER: May I go in?

COLTON: Ain't my house.

(JENNIFER struggles up steps with her suitcase. She stops at door and clears throat. COLTON stares.)

JENNIFER: Can you please get the door for me?

COLTON: I might could.

JENNIFER: What does "might could" mean?

COLTON: It might be "yes," could be "no."

(COLTON opens door for her. She exits into house with suitcase while COLTON stares at her ass and moves in sexual gesture. He discards debris from porch into yard.)

(JENNIFER steps out onto porch, sipping through water bottle straw. COLTON, not seeing her, injures thumb with hammer.)

COLTON: Shit, damn it!

(COLTON sucks his thumb. JENNIFER makes slurp sound through straw, causing COLTON to quickly pull his thumb from his mouth.)

COLTON: Nice straw ya suckin' on.

JENNIFER: Nice thumb "ya suckin' on."

COLTON: You ain't from 'round here.

JENNIFER: You think?

COLTON: Sweet Benz you drivin' there. You from up north?

JENNIFER: Smarter than you look.

(COLTON walks to JENNIFER, stands face to face, almost touching her.)

COLTON: I need to be where you are.

JENNIFER: Pardon me?

(COLTON kneels, reaches around JENNIFER'S lower legs and grabs Mt. Dew bottle. He stands, spits into bottle, walks away, resumes working.)

(JENNIFER looks at COLTON with disgust, pulls out mobile phone and calls.)

JENNIFER: Luns? I'm standing on your front porch with your ... handyman. You are coming back soon. Right? ... Soon! Right? ... Just a minute. You need screws?

COLTON: *(Loud so Luns can hear.)* Indeed! Three inches.

JENNIFER: He needs three inches. I'll wait inside.

(JENNIFER ends call and exits inside. COLTON stares at her ass as she exits, turns up music very loud, drinks, resumes work.)

(Lights to black.)

6. LUNS' PORCH – HOURS LATER

Sound of very loud country music.

Items have been moved from porch to yard. Screen is off hinges and leaning against porch. Beer cans are scattered in the yard.

COLTON, a bit drunk, repairs screen door. LUNS enters from driveway and taps COLTON on the back. COLTON jumps.

COLTON: Fuck!

(LUNS turns off radio.)

LUNS: You drink all these?

COLTON: Gotta problem with that?

LUNS: I'm not paying you thirty dollars an hour to party.

COLTON: Shit. Thirty an hour.
(He quickly gathers beer cans into trash bag.)

LUNS: Give me a hand with the lumber.

(JENNIFER walks onto porch. Stands at distance.)

JENNIFER: Luns?

LUNS: Jennifer.

JENNIFER: Took you long enough. How are you?

LUNS: Well, you see the house.

JENNIFER: Yeah, I gave myself a tour. How is he?

LUNS: Jennifer, this is Colton, and—

JENNIFER: We met.

COLTON: Pleasure was all mine now.

JENNIFER: Can we talk?

LUNS: Sure. Let me unload the lumber and I'll meet you inside.

COLTON: I got it. You two go do what you feel the need to do now.

JENNIFER: Luns? Can you bring in my guitar? Please?

COLTON: I'll fetch it.

JENNIFER: Luns?

> *(JENNIFER exits into house as COLTON stares. COLTON winks at LUNS. LUNS holds up index finger to signal, "stop." COLTON spits into bottle. LUNS walks toward car.)*

LUNS: Oh, they didn't have two by fours.

COLTON: What did ya git?

LUNS: The closest they had were one and one-half inches by three and one-half inches.

> *(COLTON laughs.)*

LUNS: What?

COLTON: Nothin' city boy. Go talk in private with yer girl.

LUNS: She's not my—

COLTON: Oh shit. She's yer daughter?

LUNS: She is not my daughter.

COLTON: Ain't love complicated now? My lips are sealed plum shut.

(LUNS exits across yard. COLTON turns on radio loudly, walks to cooler, grabs another beer, starts to open can, pauses, does not open it. He spreads out plastic to place lumber upon. LUNS enters from driveway, carrying guitar case, exits into house and immediately re-emerges with professional camera.)

COLTON: Damn, y'all're fast.
(He exits to driveway.)

JENNIFER: *(Off stage.)* Luns? You coming?

LUNS: Just a minute.

(LUNS positions and re-positions himself for the best angle for a photo. COLTON enters carrying lumber and piles it on plastic sheet. LUNS takes several rapid-succession photos of COLTON. COLTON, like a gunslinger, draws hammer from his tool belt and threatens LUNS with it.)

COLTON: Whoa, whoa. Am I in them pictures?

LUNS: Just documenting changes.

COLTON: I don't want my fuckin' picture took!

LUNS: Sorry. I was only—

COLTON: Not now! Not never! Got it?

(LUNS exits into house. COLTON kicks a plastic bucket.)

(Lights to black.)

7. LUNS' PORCH – SAME DAY – EVENING

Electric bug zapper occasionally zaps bugs. Screen door is back on hinges. A few boards are sawed, no beer cans in sight.

COLTON slaps mosquitos, puts on shirt. LUNS, carrying a glass and bottle of wine, steps out onto porch.

LUNS: Colton? You're still here.

COLTON: You should git some Citronella. Yer bug fryer ain't doin' shit.

LUNS: Looking good out here. Wow. Eleven hours.

COLTON: Uh huh.

(LUNS sips wine. COLTON packs away tools.)

COLTON: How's that wine treatin' ya?

LUNS: Oh ... uh, good. Malbec.
(Reads from bottle.)
"Argentina. Catena 1997." Would you like a glass? Now that you're finishing up.

COLTON: Nah. I gotta few cold ones left.

LUNS: Jennifer and I grilled pork chops on the back porch. Mighty tasty. You're more than welcome to help yourself.

COLTON: I'll take it home.

LUNS: Uh ... Take two plates if you like.

COLTON: All right.

(LUNS sits on porch edge and drinks. COLTON holds up a beer as if asking "okay?")

LUNS: You're off the clock. Indeed.

(COLTON pops open beer, sits next to LUNS. They drink with simultaneous movements.)

COLTON: Feels good to work. Been a while.

JENNIFER: *(Steps out onto porch.)* Luns? I'm putting the ... oh pardon me. Hi Colton. I'm putting the left overs in the fridge. Where's your aluminum foil?

LUNS: Don't worry about it. I'm fixing—"making" a couple of plates for uh ... for our neighbors.

JENNIFER: Nice. I'll hop in the shower.

LUNS: Towels in the hall closet.

JENNIFER: *(Exiting into house.)* Looks nice, Colton.

LUNS: You working for me tomorrow?

COLTON: You want me to?

LUNS: Porch won't finish itself.

COLTON: I'll be here.

LUNS: The stories this porch could tell. When I was seven, I carved my name and my friend Tony's name on that shutter. Thought it was cool as could be. Brand new pocket knife. Next day? Names were gone. Just plain not there. Dad had reversed the shutters. I took it he didn't approve of my friend. I got the nerve and asked him. He said, "Yer mama would'a had my ass had she found what you did to her new shutters. 'Specially knowin' you did it with the pocket knife she told me not to give ya."

COLTON: My first knife was a Buck Canoe.

LUNS: Buck Canoe? Mine too.

COLTON: No shit?

LUNS: No shit.

(JENNIFER steps onto porch, carrying two plates covered with aluminum foil.)

JENNIFER: Here you go. Two plates for your neighbors.

LUNS: Oh, you didn't have to ... Thank you. Colton? Do you mind dropping these down the street to the uh ... uh ...

COLTON: The Marshalls.

LUNS: The Marshalls.

COLTON: They'll appreciate this. See ya tomorrow.

(COLTON exits through yard as LUNS watches him leave. JENNIFER watches LUNS watch.)

JENNIFER: The Marshalls, huh?

LUNS: I need some more wine.

JENNIFER: I tell you what you don't need more of. Pork chops.

LUNS: What exactly are you insinuating, girl?

JENNIFER: Girl? I ain't insinuating nothin', Porkchop. You need to go on a juice diet. Like yesterday.

(JENNIFER exits into house. LUNS examines his waist roll.)

(Lights to black.)

8. SANTEE DELTA BAR AND GRILL – NIGHT

LUNS, sitting at table, washes hands with hand sanitizer.
ANGIE serves platter of oysters and a shucking knife.

ANGIE: Here. You know how'da shuck oysters?

LUNS: I grew up here.

ANGIE: You know how'da shuck oysters?

LUNS: I know how to shuck oysters.
   (He struggles shucking.)
   Ouch.

ANGIE: Uh huh! Ya wanna Corona?

LUNS: No thank you. I'm on a juice diet.

ANGIE: Juice diet?

   (LUNS struggles with oyster.)

LUNS: Ouch.
   (He sucks on finger.)

ANGIE: Juice and oysters?

LUNS: Not supposed to have oysters.

ANGIE: So you ain't on yer "juice diet."

LUNS: Okay. Give me a Corona.

ANGIE: Uh huh.
   (She opens beer bottle, serves it to LUNS, adding lime
   slice on top.)
   Here ya go. With yer juice on top.

LUNS: *(To self.)* A bit disproportionate, but thank you.

(ANGIE returns to bar as COLTON enters without seeing LUNS.)

COLTON: Angie! You seen that fag Will 'round here?

(ANGIE clears throat and nods toward LUNS.)

COLTON: Oh, hey Luns. Did ya?

ANGIE: What'da ya want with Will?

COLTON: He borrowed my lawn mower an' clippers "fer an hour" and ain't brung'em back fer two days.

ANGIE: Ya try his grandma's?

COLTON: A'course.

ANGIE: Wyonna's?

COLTON: A'course.

ANGIE: Then I'd say Will's laid up drunk somewheres.

COLTON: I need'em.
(He stares at Luns shucking.)
Fuck, Luns. Ain't never shucked no oyster, ole boy? Gimme that 'fore you kill yer self.
(He sits with LUNS, pulls out his knife to shuck.)
This here's how ya shuck. You look like a fag doin' it that'a way.

LUNS: Fags in New York Oyster Bars are shucking pros.

COLTON: At's funny, Luns. Real funny. Here. Swallow that down.

(LUNS pours fluid from shell onto ice.)

COLTON: Don't pour out the juices. You can't taste the sea.

(He shucks another oyster, pours liquid from it into LUNS' oyster.)
There ya go.

(LUNS swallows oyster.)

LUNS: Mmmm.

COLTON: Can I have one?

(LUNS motions for COLTON to eat. COLTON starts to eat, but then gives it to LUNS. He opens a second oyster. They toast with oysters and swallow and savor.)

LUNS: You swallow like a pro in a New York Oyster bar.

(ANGIE chuckles and then hides her face when COLTON looks at her.)

COLTON: Meanin' I'm a fag?

LUNS: No.

COLTON: I ain't no fag.

LUNS: I didn't say you were.

(COLTON yells and threatens LUNS with knife.)

COLTON: I ain't!

LUNS: I know, I know.

(COLTON hurriedly exits.)

LUNS: Wow.

ANGIE: Colt's touchy 'bout that.

LUNS: No shit.

ANGIE: His stepdaddy ... Nothin'.

(She exits into kitchen.)

(Lights to black.)

9. LUNS SITTING IN CHAIR IN LIMBO

Sound of EKG monitor beeping regular heart rhythm.

LUNS: The detective said that all she found was that your surgeon removed a small piece of plastic from your skull. Looked like it could be from a heavy-duty flashlight. Nothing more she can do for us.

(Pause.)

Jennifer's up in Port Indigo. Promised she'd visit you soon ... I took these photos.

(As if showing photos to Jay.)

This one's nice. You'd like to paint it.

(Pause.)

What the fuck am I doing? Sitting here talking to you like you're going to get up and say, "Yeah. That's a lovely photo, puddin'. I'll paint it naked, let you drink wine and watch. You like that? Then I'll fuck you."

(He abruptly stands.)

Wake up, God damn it! I need you to tell me who the fuck did this! I swear to God I'll hunt him down if it's the last thing I do. You got that? I know you hear me! Don't you die on me and leave me down here. You gotta see what I do to this boy.

INTERMISSION

34

ACT TWO

10. LUNS' PORCH – NOON

On the porch, there is an end table with a lamp.

COLTON works in the yard. LUNS enters from drive, carrying a fast-food bag and dragging his small roller suitcase.

LUNS: Back from Charleston. Got us some lunch.

COLTON: You know me. Always hungry.

LUNS: Let's eat in the kitchen.

COLTON: Uh ... I'll eat out here.

LUNS: Thought the three of us could eat together.

> *(COLTON quickly places a board across two saw horses, moves three folding lawn chairs to the make-shift table.)*

COLTON: There.

LUNS: Outside dining. Cheeseburgers.

> *(LUNS arranges the burgers into three piles of two each. COLTON gets two beers, holds one out for LUNS.)*

COLTON: Cold one?

LUNS: Uh ....

COLTON: It's lunch break.

LUNS: Sure.

> *(JENNIFER steps onto porch from inside house.)*

LUNS: Hi Jen. Got you a couple of burgers.

JENNIFER: Oh, Luns, you're a sweetheart, but I don't do fast food.

COLTON: Shit. More fer us.

(COLTON grabs burgers and holds one up for LUNS.)

JENNIFER: There goes your juice diet.

LUNS: Two's plenty, thanks.

JENNIFER: I'll heat up some soup. Is your microwave complicated?

COLTON: How complicated can it be? It's jest a fuckin' microwave.

LUNS: Set the timer, mash the top right button.

JENNIFER: Mash?

LUNS AND COLTON: Push!

JENNIFER: "Mash."
(She exits into house.)

LUNS: "Mash." Now I sound like my father. Let's dig in.

COLTON: Hold on now. Let's say grace.

(COLTON signals by snapping fingers and extending his hands for LUNS to hold both hands. LUNS hesitates, joins both hands with COLTON. COLTON closes his eyes, bows head, speaks without looking up.)

COLTON: Close yer eyes.

LUNS: Oh yeah.
(He closes his eyes.)

COLTON: They closed?

LUNS: Closed.

COLTON: Dear Lord, our heavenly Father. We are gathered here today in yer presence. We thank ya fer giving us this time with friends and bless those who are not able to join us.

(LUNS opens his eyes and studies COLTON. JENNIFER quietly opens screen door and snaps a photo of COLTON and LUNS. LUNS sees her and she steps back into house.)

COLTON: By yer will we are able to receive and share this bountiful meal fer which ya have so blessedly provided fer us. Help us Father to use this food fer strength to carry out yer will. In Jesus' name, amen.

(When LUNS doesn't respond, COLTON clears his throat.)

LUNS: Amen.
(He maintains a grip on COLTON'S hands.)

LUNS: You didn't ask for forgiveness.

COLTON: Fer what?

(LUNS cleans his hands with sanitizer, offers some to COLTON, who refuses.)

LUNS: I ordered two with no onion, like you eat at the Delta.

COLTON: Pay close attention, do we Lunsford?

LUNS: Indeed.

COLTON: What the hell do you do down there in Charleston?

LUNS: Slave market, houses, streets. America's beginnings. I have photos spread across the floor inside. Take a look.

COLTON: You spend a lotta time in New York?

LUNS: I do.

COLTON: Heard lots 'bout them subways.

LUNS: What did you hear about "them" subways?

COLTON: They as dangerous as folks say they is?

LUNS: Little children ride them to school.

COLTON: That's what I figured.

LUNS: Good and bad are ubiquitous.

COLTON: Huh?

LUNS: Ubiquitous. Everywhere.

COLTON: Oh. See, to me now, the Delta here is peaceful. Crickets, tree frogs, gaters sunnin' on logs.

LUNS: My friends' hearts would jump out of their chests if they saw a gater on a log.

COLTON: See, that's the problem now. People come to a place that's a million years old an' try to change it instead'a doin' right by it. You wouldn't go kick a hornets' nest or stick yer hand in a bed'a water moccasins, would ya?

(LUNS shakes head no.)

LUNS: What would you do in New York?

COLTON: I heard ya can find anything ya want there. First thing I wanna find is that buildin' where King Kong wuz.

LUNS: Empire State Building.

COLTON: See. They should'a never took that monkey outta the jungle. Shoot. I'd gone loco too. That woman wuz purty.

LUNS: Have you been with a pretty woman?

COLTON: Aaah. You caught me.

LUNS: Tell me.

COLTON: There wuz this one. Eighth grade. Prettiest thing. Used to walk her home. We'd skip school, go to the river.

LUNS: And?

COLTON: Women don't love the same as men.

(LUNS abruptly gets up from table, steps away, stands with his back to COLTON, and goes into a daze.)

COLTON: You got ketchup?

LUNS: Ketchup?

COLTON: My fries.

LUNS: Uh ... In the bag.

COLTON: You got kids?

LUNS: No ... You?

COLTON: Naw ... Quit livin' in yer head, Luns. That's a dangerous place.

(LUNS suddenly exits into house. He returns with his hands behind his back and walks to table. COLTON seeing this, suddenly on guard, slides his chair away from table, stands, and places his hand on the knife handle on his belt. LUNS reveals a 5x7 framed photo wrapped in plain brown paper and places it on table.)

COLTON: I'm suppos'd to do what with this?

(LUNS nods for COLTON to open gift. COLTON unsheathes his knife and cuts wrapping paper. He jabs the knife into the table and pulls out gift photo.)

COLTON: That's me ... I ain't seen no picture'a me since ... since ...
(He shakes his head to banish thoughts. He sits.)

LUNS: Since your school year books?

COLTON: On picture days I skipped.

LUNS: It's yours.

(COLTON locks eyes with LUNS, stares at photo, preciously rewraps it, places it face-down, eats.)

COLTON: Yer food's gittin' cold.

(Lights to black.)

11. SANTEE DELTA BAR AND GRILL – DAY

ANGIE, behind counter, adds up bills. COLTON, sitting at a table, writes on a piece of paper. His phone is on the table.

TJ: *(Offstage.)* Yeah, yeah, yeah, Will, you redneck pecker head!

(TJ enters from pool hall, carrying a cue.)

TJ: *(Yells back into pool hall.)* You couldn't beat my grandma. And she's in a fuckin' wheelchair!

(TJ laughs and then sees COLTON writing and chewing on a black pen.)

TJ: Whoa. Lookee here. What you doin', darlin'?

COLTON: What the hell's it look like?

TJ: Stuffin' black things in yer mouth as usual.

(TJ approaches COLTON and whispers.)

TJ: Hey buddy, I need two bags for Charles T. He's gittin' antsy.

COLTON: Ain't got none.

TJ: Serious now.

COLTON: I been busy in case you ain't noticed.

TJ: Yer jokin', right?

COLTON: TJ? Go play with your stick some more and leave me be in peace.

TJ: Hey! When'd'chu git a phone like mine? How the hell do ya text if ya can't read?

COLTON: Yer mama taught me in sixth grade.

(COLTON drages his index finger beneath TJ's nose to smell. TJ slaps his hand away.)

TJ: Shit Colt. Git some new material. How much Luns payin' you?

COLTON: Thirty.

TJ: An hour? Fuck. You need help?

COLTON: Nope.

TJ: Ask'im fer me.

COLTON: Nope.

TJ: Me and you always team up.

COLTON: Nope.

TJ: I need money, Colt.

(COLTON looks at text on phone, stands, places money on bar.)

COLTON: Ride's here.

TJ: Yer what?!

COLTON: Ride. Bo.

TJ: Bo? Bo charges.

COLTON: I got money.

TJ: I'll take ya where ya want. Free.

COLTON: But you don't never, do you? Bo's dependable.

TJ: I'm dependable.

COLTON: You ain't been dependable since ya learned to whack off.

(TJ blocks COLTON'S exit.)

COLTON: Git the fuck outta my way.

(TJ moves, COLTON exits.)

TJ: *(To ANGIE.)* I don't do it that much now. Really.

ANGIE: Jesus fix it. I don't need to know.
(She counts money from COLTON.)

TJ: What'd he give ya? A nickel tip?

ANGIE: Five dollar.

TJ: Boy's gone mad.

ANGIE: First time in his life I knowed Colt to stick with somethin'.

TJ: Luns's brain washin' yer cousin.

ANGIE: I git tips.

TJ: I don't trust Luns. Sneaky bastard.

ANGIE: You think they talk?

TJ: Who?

ANGIE: Luns and Colt!

TJ: How the fuck should I know what they do? You gittin' paranoid, Ang?

ANGIE: Jest askin'.

TJ: Colt's my best friend. He's mean as a snake, but he ain't no snitch.

ANGIE: Better not be.

(TJ grabs ANGIE'S shoulder.)

TJ: Meanin' 'xactly what?

(ANGIE takes TJ's hand and in controlled manner slowly pushes his hand to his chest. Talks in slow, controlled manner.)

ANGIE: Meanin' he better not be no snitch. Same goes fer you, Tracy James. Now go chalk Will's cue so I can concentrate on my accountin'.

TJ: Jesus Christ.

ANGIE: Better not let Colt hear you sayin' that.

TJ: Colt ain't never here no more, now is he?

(TJ exits as ANGIE blankly stares and then resumes counting.)

(Lights to black.)

12. LUNS' PORCH – DAY – NEXT DAY

On the porch are JENNIFER'S *guitar, a large abstract painting of the guitar on an easel, paintbrushes, a paint palate, and* LUNS' *coat hanging over the railing.*

COLTON, sitting alone on porch steps, is crying. LUNS enters from inside the house. COLTON quickly wipes tears, composes.

LUNS: What's the matter?

COLTON: Nothin'.

LUNS: Anything I can do?

(COLTON shakes head no. LUNS sits on steps but remains distant.)

LUNS: I can listen.

COLTON: Life.

LUNS: Yeah. Life.

COLTON: My ma smashed the photo you give me ... I can't picture you ever being mean.

LUNS: I'd like to believe that.

(COLTON stands and resumes porch work.)

COLTON: You made it outta here. New York.

LUNS: I did.

COLTON: I'm gonna go to New York ... When I first met Jennifer, I acted like you and her ... I git nasty sometimes.

LUNS: It's okay.

COLTON: You gotta wife up there? Girlfriend?

LUNS: No one special.

COLTON: Nobody at all?

LUNS: I was in love. But there was a ... an incident and, and uh ... that was the last person I'll ever hug. The last time I'll be so close to smell ... someone I love.

COLTON: Shit ... Sorry. Hope I didn't cast no bad spell on ya, and make ya think there's no love left.
(Pause.)
That's a nice painting.

LUNS: Jennifer is indeed talented.

COLTON: When I git money, I'ma buy me a paintin'.

(As COLTON works, LUNS stares ahead for a moment and then walks into house. He returns with two beers and a small painting of fishing boats. Hands beer to COLTON.)

COLTON: What'ya got there?

LUNS: An old painting. Boats.

COLTON: Who painted it?

LUNS: A friend ... very good friend.

COLTON: Instead of payin' me git yer very good friend to paint me one.

(COLTON picks up painting, looks at it. He resumes work.)

(Sound of mobile phone ring.)

LUNS: *(Answers phone.)* Hello ... Yes, this is he ... just a minute.
(He moves into yard.)
So what are you telling me? South Carolina doesn't recognize our rights? It's legal in New York ... Don't tell me I don't have options. I have options! What the fuck good are ya'll boys? You're a major university hospital for Christ's sake!
(He ends call and storms toward porch.)
Fuckin' inbred hicks!
(He walks onto porch, kicks over chair.)
God damn it!

(LUNS wheezes, can hardly catch his breath. COLTON goes to LUNS' coat hanging on railing and gets LUNS' inhaler. LUNS breathes through the inhaler, exits into house.)

(COLTON places chair upright with care.)

(Lights to black.)

13. LUNS' PORCH – NIGHT – DAYS LATER

Porch has improvements, the shutters painted and hung. LUNS, sitting in porch chair, reads a book. JENNIFER steps from house onto porch.

JENNIFER: How did your meeting go with Dr. Taymor?

LUNS: Jay doesn't have a living will. Legally, at least in New York, I'm his first of kin. Down here? Naw. Dr. Taymor is talking with the University Hospital Legal Team.

JENNIFER: Ridiculous. You're his husband.
(She pours glass of wine, sips it, walks to shutters, opens and closes them.)
These look nice.

LUNS: Colt hung them a few days back.

JENNIFER: There are names on this one.

LUNS: What?

JENNIFER: On the back. "Jeremy plus Tony."

LUNS: I thought he painted over them.
(He walks to shutter and inspects it.)
The bugger re-carved them.

JENNIFER: Who are Jeremy and Tony?

LUNS: People from forty ... plus years ago. Jeremy, that's me, first name, actually Jeremiah.

JENNIFER: "Jeremiah?"

LUNS: Tony Spano. Greek kid.

JENNIFER: And?

LUNS: I was in second grade. Tony was the junior-high football star. My hero. When my old man died, Tony helped mom with this place. He passed football with me, took me camping.

JENNIFER: Camping?

LUNS: I had my Greek god all to myself. With every breath I watched his sleeping bag rise and lower. Us sharing the same air.

JENNIFER: Nice.

LUNS: Tony, like all Greek gods, slept in the nude.

JENNIFER: Nicer.

LUNS: Behave. I carefully lifted Tony's unzipped sleeping bag cover. Peeped. He woke. Scared the shit out of me. He smiled. Opened his bag. I climbed in. I put my arm around his waist. Slept that way all night.

JENNIFER: And?

LUNS: The most peaceful ... moment of my life.

JENNIFER: That was it?!

LUNS: *(Pause.)* If the legal team agrees, Dr. Taymor wants me to pull the plug.

(JENNIFER buries her head in her hands, cries lightly. LUNS hugs her. She looks up.)

JENNIFER: I'll go with you.

(Lights to black.)

14. LUNS' PORCH – NIGHT – DAY LATER

Lamp on end table is turned on. There is a cake sitting on the porch.

COLTON cleans yard, looks around to see if anyone is looking, sneaks Jennifer's guitar out of case. Sits in yard and softly plays guitar as he sings "Colton's Tune."

Early during the song, LUNS quietly steps onto the porch, holding an aluminum-covered pan and two beers. He quietly watches COLTON.

COLTON: *(Plays guitar and sings.)*

There's a strong sea wind blowin,'
Hummin' through my heart.

(He shakes his head no, scratches out word, writes new word, sings.)

Chorus:
There's a strong sea wind blowin,'
Whistlin' through my heart.
With sea waves floodin'
Far as I can see,
And that cold wind chill keeps slappin' hard,
Numbin' round my heart,
Drownin' out what good I'd found,
Tearin' me apart.

Verse One:
Took our old drive-in movie screen,
Where I learned to kiss,
Took the church where I tried to pray,
For the folks I miss.

Repeat Chorus
There's a strong wind blowin,' …. Tearin' me apart.

Verse Two:
Took the tree where our names wuz carved,
And the dock we fished.
Took the truck where I first made love,
Stole the dreams I wished.

Repeat Chorus
There's a strong wind blowin,' …. Tearin' me apart.

Tearin' me apart.

(COLTON, seeing LUNS, stops. LUNS places the pan on the porch and opens beers.)

LUNS: Good stuff happening out here. Here's some ribs for you and for uh …

COLTON: Mom. I'll drop a plate for her.

(They drink beers.)

LUNS: Was that original?

COLTON: We need more two by fours.

LUNS: You mean "one and a halfs" by "three and a halfs."

COLTON: Yeah those ones.

LUNS: I'll run pick'em up. Go get my money. Living room desk. Top drawer.

COLTON: *(Anxious.)* Inside?

LUNS: Colton? By now I hoped you'd feel enough pride to feel at home here. Top drawer.

(COLTON hesitates, exits into house. After a moment he rapidly emerges from inside and hurriedly exits through yard. LUNS calmly sips beer, not responding to COLTON.)

(JENNIFER, fairly intoxicated, emerges from house with a bottle of wine and two glasses.)

JENNIFER: He forgot his ribs.

LUNS: He could have sat here, talked. It had to be one way or the other.

JENNIFER: There's a lamp on your porch.

LUNS: First a lamp, later a baggy sofa, later a TV. Southerners live on porches. Only go inside for suspicious activities.

JENNIFER: It's attracting mosquitos.
(She looks closely at cake and reads icing.)
Where did this heavy sugar-frosted cake come from? "Welcome Home Jeremy."

LUNS: Colt's mom. She wants to hook up with me.

JENNIFER: With a store bought cake?

LUNS: She never had a clue how to plan ahead.

JENNIFER: At least "Colt" comes by it honestly. Want some Shiraz?

LUNS: I have beer.

JENNIFER: I watched you drink bottle after bottle of fine wines. Now? "I have beer." Where the hell am I?
(She pours wine and sips.)
I nosed around your study. Jay did some nice paintings while he was down here.

LUNS: The Hamilton Plantation, a fire tower, shrimp boats.

JENNIFER: An abstract of this house. Supposed to be a birthday surprise.

LUNS: He didn't know where I grew up.

JENNIFER: Nosy Jay?

LUNS: Shit ... I had assumed he was in Atlanta. Having an affair.

JENNIFER: An affair?

LUNS: His love was not faithful.
(Pause.)
Did you two ever ... ?

JENNIFER: He's queer.

LUNS: Yes or no?

JENNIFER: You have no right to—

LUNS: Did you fuck my husband? Straight forward question.

JENNIFER: No!

LUNS: You're lying.

JENNIFER: Fuck you.

LUNS: How many times?

JENNIFER: Six, seven, I don't know.

LUNS: Back when you two first "painted together?"

JENNIFER: Nothing regular.

LUNS: Glad it was "nothing regular."

JENNIFER: Only when we got high.

LUNS: That makes me feel better.

JENNIFER: He said you were in love with someone else.

LUNS: What?!

JENNIFER: Tim.

LUNS: Tim who?

JENNIFER: Some photography student.

LUNS: I don't fuck my students.

JENNIFER: He didn't say you fucked. He said you loved someone.

LUNS: I love all my students. Jay obviously carried it a bit further.

JENNIFER: I was never his student!

LUNS: Pardon me. Apprentice.

JENNIFER: Jay and I had everything in common. Unlike anyone I've ever known.

LUNS: He was my husband. My love.

JENNIFER: He was my ... my—

LUNS: Soulmate?

(JENNIFER nods.)

LUNS: Want a list of all the people who said that? "Oh Jay is my soulmate." "Oh Jay sees only me." "Jay really understands."

JENNIFER: That was his gift.

LUNS: He could fill card catalogues of men and women he gave his gifts to.

JENNIFER: I don't care. In our moments there were only the two of us. What he did with his other moments? I don't give a fuck.

LUNS: Modernist morality.

JENNIFER: You know what pissed him off about you?

LUNS: He told you or you're an omniscient wonder?

JENNIFER: He fucking told me!

(LUNS motions for JENNIFER to share.)

JENNIFER: He was pissed that you were so fucking faithful.

LUNS: Faithful? In your and Jay's moral view "faithful" is a disease?

JENNIFER: You two were never on the same page.

LUNS: 'Cause I never had "an affair?"

(JENNIFER shakes her head in disgust.)

LUNS: Well I did.

JENNIFER: Bullshit.

LUNS: I did.

JENNIFER: You did not.

LUNS: Back in New York while Jay was down here.

JENNIFER: Oh. My. God.

LUNS: Unplanned … the UPS guy.

JENNIFER: Vinnie?

(LUNS turns away. JENNIFER breaks into laughter.)

LUNS: It's not funny, Jen.

JENNIFER: Oh my God, oh my God. Vinnie in his little brown shorts?

LUNS: Stop it.

JENNIFER: I drooled over Vinnie.

LUNS: Who didn't?

JENNIFER: God he's gorgeous.

LUNS: I am trying to feel guilt over here.

(JENNIFER hugs LUNS and laughs.)

JENNIFER: Welcome to the real world, Lunsford.

(LUNS refuses to return hug. He stands and steps away.)

JENNIFER: Where are you going?

(LUNS steps into house. He returns holding folded pieces of paper and sits.)

JENNIFER: What's that?

LUNS: A deed. I had thought of leaving this house to … to uh … but …

(LUNS holds lighter near the papers to burn them.)

(Lights to black.)

15. SANTEE DELTA BAR AND GRILL – MORNING

ANGIE cleans glasses at bar while COLTON is slumped on a table from previous night. TJ enters, walks to COLTON and wakes him.

COLTON: *(Groaning.)* Ah shit.

TJ: You look like death.

ANGIE: I found him sleepin' out on the dock.

(COLTON pulls photo from pocket and hands it to TJ.)

TJ: *(Whispers.)* Where the fuck did you get this?

COLTON: Sssh. Luns' desk.

TJ: That's the fag we … how come Luns is at the hospital with that boy?

COLTON: They's both from New York. I don't know.

(ANGIE walks to TJ and COLTON. TJ tries to hide photo. ANGIE snaps fingers and gestures "hand that to me." COLTON pulls photo from TJ and gives to ANGIE.)

ANGIE: Where the fuck did y'all git this?

TJ: He got it at Luns'.

(ANGIE walks to bar, pours herself a shot of whiskey, stares at photo, slams drink.)

TJ: *(Whispers.)* What'll we do?

ANGIE: TJ, you're as dumb as they come. Nobody's here. Quit fuckin' whisperin'.

TJ: What the fuck's yer problem?

ANGIE: Ya'll boys are my fuckin' problem. Colt works fer a guy with a picture of the faggot y'all beat! Showed up snoopin' after y'all skull fucked that pink flamingo! Oh, and by the way? There wuz a detective sniffin' 'round 'fore Luns come.

TJ: What the fuck did you tell him?

ANGIE: I ain't told'er shit. You think I'd run my mouth 'bout what happened?

TJ: You told us to take yer pickup.

ANGIE: Not drag him! And I said, "dump him in the swamp." Not "near" the swamp.

TJ: How wuz we suppose'ta know Will's sister'd be out there in the swamp fuckin' Reverend Ted?

ANGIE: Retards.

TJ: We wuz tryin' to cover fer Colt.

ANGIE: You can't even cover yer own ass, Tracy James.

(TJ grabs ANGIE and pins her against the bar. COLTON jumps up, grabs TJ by the collar and they fight.)

ANGIE: Ya'll boys ...

(The fight ends in a standoff.)

TJ: I should not never listen to you or yer fuckin' cousin.

(TJ exits. COLTON goes to bar, pours a drink, slams it.)

ANGIE: How'd ya git that picture?

COLTON: It wuz in his desk.

ANGIE: Is Luns a cop? Wuz the nigger boy a cop?

COLTON: I'm assumin' they wuz friends. I think yer woman detective works fer Luns. They gotta be onto us.

ANGIE: They ain't got proof. But if that boy lives, we got problems.

COLTON: Ya think he'll live?

ANGIE: He's on a ventilator. Said so in this mornin's *Post and Courier.*
(She hands newspaper to COLTON.)
Go find out who he is.

COLTON: We know who Luns is.

ANGIE: No we don't! You gotta take care'a this now.

COLTON: I can't do it. There's something goin' on with Luns.

ANGIE: What'da ya mean somethin' goin' on?

COLTON: I'm jest tellin' ya. I ain't doin' this one.

ANGIE: I knew it wuz only a matter'a time.

COLTON: What'chu jest say?

ANGIE: Faggot.

(COLTON punches her like he's punching a man, laying ANGIE flat on her back.)

COLTON: You wanna act like a man? I'll treat ya like a man. You do what you see fit, but I'm out.

(COLTON exits. ANGIE slowly stands and cleans face. She slams a shot. Calls on mobile phone.)

ANGIE: TJ? We got a problem we gotta fix ... Think you can git Will and Randy and meet me and Colt at the plantation? ... Good. We'll do what we gotta do.

(Lights to black.)

16. LUNS' PORCH – THE NEXT DAY – DUSK

LUNS and JENNIFER walk from driveway to porch. LUNS carries a large folder of papers and a hospital personal belongings bag. They sit. LUNS pulls Jay's pink, bloodied shirt from the bag and smells it. He kisses the shirt and strokes it gently, and places it back in the bag.

JENNIFER: Are you going to be all right? ... If I were in a coma, I would want someone who loved me as much as you love Jay to ... help me.

LUNS: "To find peace?" The social worker handed me a pamphlet saying that thinking how you are being kind, loving, helpful ... jerking out the God damn plug makes it easier. What the fuck do pamphlet writers know? *(He pulls Jay's watch from bag, looks at it, puts it on.)* His watch is broken. Two-thirty-seven a.m.

JENNIFER: I can stay longer.

(LUNS shakes his head "no.")

JENNIFER: My suitcase is in the car. I just need my guitar.

(JENNIFER exits into house. COLTON, in church clothes, walks up to house and stands near porch.)

LUNS: Where have you been?

COLTON: Church.

LUNS: Praying for forgiveness?

(COLTON pulls photo from pocket, hands it to LUNS, backs away.)

LUNS: You brought back my photo.

COLTON: Y'all worked together?

LUNS: No ... You were at the Delta that night.

(COLTON stares at ground. LUNS looks at photo, lays it on porch, and exits into house. COLTON paces in yard. LUNS emerges with two beers, holds out one to COLTON. COLTON approaches and takes beer. LUNS sits on top porch step and drinks.)

COLTON: I read 'bout yer friend James in the paper. He doin' all right?

LUNS: I call him, "Jay." I unplugged his ventilator this morning.

(JENNIFER emerges onto porch, carrying guitar case.)

JENNIFER: You sure you don't want me to stay?

(LUNS shakes head "no.")

JENNIFER: Well ...
(She pats LUNS on shoulder and walks toward car.)

COLTON: Jen?

JENNIFER: Yeah, Colt?

COLTON: I'll be seein' ya in New York.

JENNIFER: I'll take you out for a Bud. I know a great place where we can see the whole city.

COLTON: The Empire State Buildin'?

JENNIFER: Yes and no.

COLTON: What's that mean?

JENNIFER: Yes and no? It means "might could."

COLTON: *(Laughs.)* Ahhh. You got me good.

(JENNIFER resumes walking away.)

COLTON: Jen? Sorry I wuz rude to ya at first.

(JENNIFER smiles.)

COLTON: I can carry yer guitar.

JENNIFER: That would be nice.

(JENNIFER hands guitar case to COLTON and they exit together. LUNS remains motionless on porch. COLTON returns with case.)

COLTON: She give me this. Said you told her I wuz musically inclined. Thank you, Luns.
(He sits on edge of porch, distant from LUNS.)
Sorry 'bout yer friend.

LUNS: What'chu got to be sorry fer?

COLTON: I had this dog one time. Rodney. Mutt always got into our trash, everybody's trash. Every few days – big mess. The whole neighborhood blamed me. So, this one day he got in our trash, dragged dead fish an' ole oyster shells all over our porch. I lost it. Hit Rodney with a shovel. Jest meant to teach'im a lesson, you know, not hurt'im. But I broke his ribs. He couldn't breath. I wudn't leave him like that, you know? So I ... I loved that mutt.

LUNS: I met Jay at a Broadway play. We had seats next to one another. What were the chances? *Bent.* About homosexual men in a Nazi concentration camp. Treated even worse than the Jews. Jay whispered, "That's me. Homosexual and Jewish." I didn't even know him and there in that Broadway theatre, he whispered his

entire life to me. Black, homosexual, and Jewish. Back then I didn't tell anything to anyone.
(He picks up photo and looks at it.)
What did you do to my husband?

COLTON: I seen him in the Delta, a negro man drinking by his self. Pink Polo shirt, khaki shorts, dockers. Drinkin' "Blue Moon with a slice'a orange." Not from the Delta. He thought he wuz slick, wearin' them sunglasses inside, checkin' us out without us knowin' it. Second time he come in, he bought a round fer the whole damn bar. One round turned to three. So we invited him over to shoot pool. Pissed off Will that yer friend ... husband hustled us. He won a shit load more than them shots cost. Gotta bag'a pot off TJ. Never paid'im.

LUNS: And the last time?

COLTON: We had ran up to Myrtle Beach to set up this carnival. Drinkin' all day. We come into the Delta already drunk and there wuz "flamingo boy." Randy called'im that cuz'a all his pink shirts. Yer friend wuz gabbin' at Angie.

LUNS: Jay.

COLTON: Jay went to the shitter. Angie yells at me, "Colton, me and yer colorful boyfriend wuz jest talkin' 'bout how much we wuz both missin' yer purty face. He set here being all lonely cuz you wuzn't here so I told'im you always make it. He set here waitin' his little nigger heart out fer ya." Then TJ pipes up, "Hell, Colt. Tonight you may git lucky after all." 'Bout that time yer friend stumbles outta the bathroom and come straight fer me. Puts his arm 'round me and asks me if I'd be up fer "a walk on the beach." Asks me in front'a TJ, Randy, Will, Angie. Asks me in front'a God. I shove him off and go outside to TJ's truck to smoke. All he has to do is leave me be. But he follows me. Wants to make up. Apologize with his black faggot fingers feelin' all over me. Pins me against TJ's truck. Tries'ta kiss me. I grab the Maglite and swung it. Just meant to scare'im. Then TJ come out and—

LUNS: I don't need to hear more.

(LUNS stands and exits into house. COLTON cries, paces, sits on top step. LUNS steps out onto porch, holding one beer. He walks up behind COLTON and hands beer to COLTON over COLTON'S shoulder.)

LUNS: Here you go, Colt.

COLTON: Thanks, Luns.

(LUNS sits on the porch edge behind COLTON, straddling him in a manner so he can lean forward and hug COLTON from behind. He reaches forward and pulls COLTON'S head back against his own torso, wrapping one arm around him. He hugs COLTON for a moment. COLTON shows a moment of relief, settles back into the embrace. They embrace one another, strongly crying. LUNS slowly slides his arm up to COLTON'S neck and suddenly begins a "blood choke" or "rear- naked choke hold.")

(COLTON drops his beer and struggles to pry LUNS' arm from his throat. LUNS leans back into the choke, staring upward at the sky as if praying, whispering.)

LUNS: It's okay. It's gonna be okay.

(COLTON can no longer make a sound due to the strong grip by LUNS. He struggles fiercely and pulls out his knife but is too weak to open it and drops it as he dies. After a moment, LUNS releases the chokehold and cradles COLTON'S head. He speaks in eerily cheerful tone as he rocks COLTON.)

LUNS: It's gonna be fine now. I told Jay, years ago, me and him should adopt a kid, a boy, the two of us raise a son

together. Jay flat out refused. Oh Colton buddy, we should never have drank that first cold one together ... no, that's not true. We were hot. We were thirsty. *(Pause.)*
I feel you squeezin' my hand buddy. That's good. Real good. Thank you, Colt. Thank you.

(TJ and ANGIE enter from yard.)

TJ: What the?! Two fags makin' out! No wonder you didn't meet us at the plantation, Colt. Ya'out here with yer boyfriend. We waited fer yer sorry ass three hours ... You hear what I'm sayin' to ya?

ANGIE: Hold up, TJ.
(She approaches and checks COLTON'S carotid pulse.)
Ain't got no pulse.

TJ: No pulse?! What'chu mean?

LUNS: I feel him squeezing my hand.

TJ: See Ang.

ANGIE: You ain't feelin' shit, Luns. You killed'im.

TJ: Killed'im?! No, no. That ain't—

ANGIE: Shut up Tracy James! Colton Rivers is dead! You got that?

TJ: Luns jest said—

ANGIE: Look at'im.

TJ: We gotta call an am-ba-lance or somethin'.

ANGIE: We ain't callin' shit.

TJ: We gotta help Colt.

(ANGIE slaps TJ.)

ANGIE: Now you ain't seein' this clearly. Luns jest did me and you a big favor.

LUNS: He choked.

ANGIE: Nobody blamin' you, Luns honey. Colt had it comin'.

LUNS: The doctor told me to pull the plug.

TJ: What'da we do?

ANGIE: Luns? ... Luns baby? Let go'a him.

LUNS: Huh?

ANGIE: Let go'a Colt, baby. Here TJ, help me lay Colt on the ground.

(TJ and ANGIE lift COLTON from LUNS' arms and lay him on the ground.)

ANGIE: There now.

TJ: Colt's my best friend.

ANGIE: Colt weren't never nobody's best friend. 'Specially yours. We jest all put up with'im.

TJ: He's jest layin' there.

ANGIE: Tracy James! Look at me ... Luns helped us out.

TJ: Huh?

ANGIE: Colt killed Luns' nigger friend all by his self. You got that? All – by – his – self.

TJ: All by his self.

ANGIE: It's all evened out. Luns? Luns?

(LUNS does not respond.)

ANGIE: It's okay honey. Me and TJ'll git back to what we do here and you go git back to yer photography in Spain.

LUNS: I ain't never been to Spain.

ANGIE: Course ya have, darlin'. We seen yer purty pictures.

LUNS: I tried to leave.

(LUNS talks as he exits into house.)

LUNS: I wuz never gonna come back here.

TJ: What'da we do?

ANGIE: Think Colt told Luns 'bout us?

TJ: I don't know.

ANGIE: Best we not take no chance.

TJ: He ain't gonna tell nobody. He's gotta spell on'im.

(ANGIE pulls TJ's knife from his side sheath.)

ANGIE: I ain't riskin' it. You git in that house.
(She holds up knife.)

TJ: No.

ANGIE: What the hell wuz I thinkin' askin' a boy to do a man's work? I'll git Will or Randy to do it.

(TJ snatches knife from ANGIE and exits into house. ANGIE sits on porch, and calmly smokes several drags.)

(Sounds of crickets and tree frogs.)

(TJ emerges from house, wipes knife blade on his pants.)

ANGIE: Yer gonna have to burn them pants.

TJ: They's old.

(ANGIE smokes a few puffs.)

ANGIE: Go git Will and Randy. Pull the truck 'round back. Load'em both up.

TJ: Take'em where?

ANGIE: Down to the swamp. Make sure they's in the swamp, not next to it. Figure y'all boys can do that much?

TJ: What 'bout you?

ANGIE: I'm gonna burn this fuckin' place to the ground. Should'a done that a long time ago.

(TJ exits. ANGIE, sitting calmly, smokes, then stares at COLTON'S body.)

ANGIE: What wuz you thinkin' cuz? Tryin' to leave the Delta.

ANGIE: *(Yells into house.)* You too, Luns! Y'all boys forgot we wuz family? We belong to the Delta.
(She calmly leans against post and smokes.)

(Sounds of crickets, frogs, and bug noises increase, then abruptly cease as lights abruptly go to black.)

CURTAIN

Colton's Tune

Donald Fidler

There's a strong sea wind blowin', __ whistlin' __ through my heart. __ With sea waves floodin' __ far as I can see. And that cold wind chill keeps slappin' __ hard, numbin' __ round my heart, drowin' out what good I'd found, tearin' __ me a- part. Took our

old drive in movie — screen, where I learned to kiss, took the church where I tried to pray

for the folks I miss. There's a strong sea wind blowin', — whistlin' — through my heart. — With

sea waves floodin' — far as I can see. And that cold wind chill keeps slappin' — hard,

About the Authors

Travis Teffner

Travis Teffner is a stage and film actor, from Hendersonville, North Carolina. He has also co-authored alongside DC Fidler on the plays, *Elk and Wolf* and *Moon Bugs,* and authored the play, *Over Before It Began.*

DC Fidler

A native of the South, DC Fidler has combined a career in academic psychiatry and cultural psychiatry with a lifetime of playwriting, acting, directing, composing music, and teaching creative writing and the dramatic arts.

He studied theatre, writing, chemistry, medicine, and psychiatry at the University of North Carolina at Chapel Hill, where he served on the faculty. He later served on the faculty at West Virginia University, teaching cultural psychiatry, clinical psychiatry, and acting.

A licensed psychiatrist, DC Fidler has lived and worked with the Alutiiq tribe in Akhiok, Alaska; the Al Moqbali Bedouin tribe near Sohar, Oman; the Kalkadoon Aboriginal Tribe in the outback of Queensland, Australia; and the Te Tau Ihu Maori Tribes on the South Island of New Zealand.

He began his acting career in outdoor dramas, summer stock theatre, and local films and television at age ten. He has written scripts and composed music for over fifty medical educational videos at UNC-CH and WVU. He has written twenty plays that have been produced in various community theatres and universities across North Carolina, Virginia, and West Virginia, as well as St. Louis, Sacramento, San Diego, Los Angeles, Boston, Chicago, and New York City.

He consulted and appeared in educational productions for HBO, ABC, and PBS and performed in numerous stage plays including: *Hope is the Thing with Feathers, Night of January 16th, Thieves' Carnival, Blood Wedding, Our Town, A Life in the Theatre,* and *Fool for Love.*

Presently, he is a scriptwriter, film director, and medical consultant for educational films using professional actors to demonstrate mental health issues. In addition, he is an active member of the Dramatists Guild of America and the Charlotte Writers' Club.

Fidler previously chaired the Video Committee for the American Psychiatric Association and served as President of the Association for Academic Psychiatry. In 2003, he was inducted as a Fellow of the Royal College of Physicians of Ireland. He serves on the Arts and Humanities Committee for the Group for the Advancement of Psychiatry where he is co-producing a video series on the History of Psychiatry.

He is author of the textbook, *Psychiatry for Actors: Using Psychiatric Principles to Build Characters,* and author of the novel, *Boogieban.*

Plays by DC Fidler and Travis Teffner
- Elk and Wolf
- Santee Delta
- Moon Bugs

Plays by Travis Teffner
- Over Before It Began
- Grilling

Plays by DC Fidler
- Voices in the Woods
- Guilt by Association (With RJ Casey)
- Three Diaries
- Master William Bowlinggreen and Company
- Shiraz
- The Anniversary of Miss Nanette Pringle
- School Children Hiding Under Desks
- Grams
- Camp Uni
- Boogieban (Two-Actor Version)
- Boogieban (Seven-Actor Version)
- Ahulaqs
- Celtic Crossing
- Stone Touchin'
- Daugherty Park Merry-Go-Round
- La Dynastie
- Gyges Solution
- Persons
- Cruise
- Mobile to Where
- Oman Truce
- Second Amendment
- The Greek God Club
- Four X
- Microscopic Misconceptions
- Drone Guns

Musicals by DC Fidler
- Pied Piper (With Lauren Horacek)
- Healer Man
- Medicine Show